Lines a

Megan Karr

DEDICATION

To my wonderful family; immediate, biological, and distant.

CONTENTS

AUTHOR'S NOTE

This collection of poems and short stories paints different pictures of how people today view love. However, the majority of these views are flawed in the respect that they are completely opposite of what love was intended to look like. Under each title in this collection is a word describing what kind of love is featured in the story. The last story in the collection is a modernized version of what Christ did for us all. Society today gives into the lie that true love is addictive, misunderstood, envious, record keeping, self-seeking, and dishonoring. However, Christ himself gave us a perfect depiction of love when he died for us so that one day we could spend eternity with him. Love is sacrifice, trusting, persevering, hopeful and preserving. Love never fails. God never fails. God is Love.

POEMS

CHRISTMAS
Childlike Love

A beautiful day both cheery and bright.
I'll sleep by the fire, cozy and light.
What kind of day will this winter breeze bring?
Snow all around, hear the little birds sing.
"Christmas is coming," the children say.
The feeling is warm, happy, and gay.
They sing joyful songs and gaze at the lights.
Winter is here and they love all the sights.
Music fills the air and cookies are baked.
Sweet smells and warmth, from this scene, I will take.
Hugs all around from Granny and Pops;
I never want this feeling to stop.
Love is all around and in everything.
Parents are scrambling as they watch their children gleam.
The snowflakes are falling on this Christmas eve,
and never from this sight do I want to leave.

QUILT OF MEMORIES
Practical Love

Diapers and blankets, a hospital room.
A family of people, yours to be, soon.
Animals dance over your head.
They lay you down and put you to bed.

Another piece of fabric sewn into the timeline of your life.
Stitches of good times and tear stains of bad, all together
the pieces, you see.
A quilt of memories.

Band-aids and recess.
Hair is a mess.
Elementary school at its prime.
It seems like friends will be there forever,
but you move on and catch up with time.

Another piece of fabric sewn into the timeline of your life.
Stitches of good times and tear stains of bad, all together
the pieces, you see.
A quilt of memories.

Caps and gowns for a graduate.
High school and college, then, that's it?
Celebration time and a graduation commences
as feelings are heightened and flood your senses.

Another piece of fabric sewn into the timeline of your life.
Stitches of good times and tear stains of bad, all together
the pieces, you see.
A quilt of memories.

Marriage. Babies.
Retirement. Maybe.
Life flies by too fast,
as you begin wondering why you were cast.
Replacements flood in and you take one final bow,
knowing your memory will live on somehow.
The curtain closes and the lights fade,
but you are pleased because you got to dance on the stage.

Another piece of fabric sewn into the timeline of your life.
Stitches of good times and tear stains of bad, all together
the pieces, you see.
A quilt of memories.

SHE
Abusive Love

I see her there sitting all alone.
She cringes in memory of that place she called home.
Was it a dream? Maybe a nightmare?
How could she ever find love inside there?

She tried to forget all the lies she was told;
The memories and torture –she was only eight years old.
She was a gleeful girl that turned into dust.
We sit by and watch when that could have been us.

We always walk past her. We laugh every which way,
teasing and mocking her without even knowing her name.
She has been silenced through the years of bruises and hits,
You could have been friends, but it's she you'll never miss.

We carry on with our everyday woes
never even seeing this child living among foes.
She will cry every night until someone hears,
but people have been blinded and have covered their ears.

She will grow up and leave this behind her,
but she will always keep her scars as reminders.

SEA OF GLASS
Miserable Love

The tears come up and trickle down,
like acid rain in a stormy town.
They freeze and shatter like frozen ice.
I guess my heart was not enough to last,
in a sea of broken glass.

I knew if I swam in it, I would bleed.
I never expected it to scar.
The cuts are so deep from the rushing tides,
I just can't survive.

They say when glass breaks the shards still fit,
but if someone takes them away there is no point to it.
I will love you no matter what or how deep you've cut.

The tears come up and trickle down,
like acid rain in a stormy town.
They freeze and shatter like frozen ice.
I guess my heart was not enough to last,
in a sea of broken glass.

AMERICA, 2014
Non-Existent Love

Economy is on everyone's mind
as they sit down and waste their time.
The day draws to an end, but who has yet to begin?
It seems as if, to me, there is so much more to be,
than obese robots with cancer.
Does anyone have an answer?

So focused on our media,
we forget we have encyclopedias.
A summer stroll in a park, is taxing exercise on our hearts.
We hear activists screaming for equality, but refused to
recognize a child's body.
We give rights to those who can fight, but deny humans
their inalienable rights.

There is no liberty without life.
It does not matter who is wrong or right.
We seemed to have lost our place.
We bring our fore–fathers disgrace.

We will continue down this path.
Most will never look back.
However, history is vital.
We've abandoned God and chosen idols.
The answer to our problems is not here on this earth, but
somewhere in that book that people think is cursed.

THE ONE ABOUT DIVORCE
Cowardly Love

You run me over and kill my dreams,
but the memories of you will never leave.

I have tried for so long to let you go.
How can I keep putting on this show?
Yes, you are gone, and do I care?
Not really, until I see you standing there.

You ripped out my heart and chose to do this.
So, why is it you I truly miss?
You broke my heart and said you would stop,
but you twist my emotions into a mangled knot.

You said that you loved me, so why would you leave?
It seems that you love her more than you ever loved me.
Come back and face me, try being a man.
You won't, because you're not, and you never can.

MY MELODY
Professional Love

I'm searching for chords to make a song
that fits into my story.
My director leads me as I sing lyrics with no melody.
Can I compose a symphony?

The director leads me as I listen.
I close my eyes and hear the music in the distance.
He gives me the notes one by one,
the story has just begun.

I've found the chord to make a song that fits into my story.
My director leads me as I sing lyrics to His perfect melody.
Together, we composed a symphony.

THANK YOU
Resentful Love

You showed me a world filled with art and life,
but I never thanked you for all of the strife.
You gave me a reason to fight for myself,
and now I can thank you for putting me on a shelf.

Maybe you broke me, but I needed the pieces,
they helped me find someone who cared to reach us.
By us, I mean me and my feelings too.
You see, you left me critiques to find something true.

Now that I've found the thing I've been looking for
I can finally say thank you and even the score.

A LIFE IS A LIFE
An Unborn Child's Love

It is what it is. I am alive.
A person is loved. Yes, you are, but am I?
A heart is a heart, a stone is a stone.
One hit stops the beat, but I am never alone.
They made the mistake, now, why would they cry?
That person has fallen, and now I must die.
A human is a human and a bone is a bone
My life is a life, please, don't rush me home.

THAT SEPTEMBER EVE
Lacking Love

We look upon the building so dark and empty tonight.
See the mothers on their knees as they break down and cry.
They had a choice and yes, they chose.
Why this? Will anyone ever know?

There really is no choice, a life is a life.
If you really were their parents,
you'd take their place and die.
No peace, no hope, but we still go on our way.
We watch in silence as we rip our children apart everyday.

You see the father confused as he tries to pick up the
pieces, "but someone could've stared."
"What if my parents see us?"
They walk out of the building and see a small sign.
It says, "I'll take your baby. I could never have one of mine."

The mom looks to the father in shock of what they did.
Now they go on knowing their child never lived.

IT AIN'T EASY BEING ONE
Comical Love

It ain't easy being one,
when your poops the colors of the trees.
You move about on hands and knees.
It ain't easy being one.

You want to speak but can't be heard,
making noises but no words,
eating food that tastes like curds.
It ain't easy being one.

It ain't easy being one.
Getting kisses from all these hotties,
but I can't even use my potty.
It ain't easy being one.

When your life is such a chore,
and your food is on the floor,
because your morning came at four.
It ain't easy being one.

It ain't easy being one.
When you're left out in the sun.
They keep you from all the fun.
It ain't easy being one.

You have no choice of where to go.
All they say to you is no.
Where you'll wake, you never know.
It ain't easy being one.

So next time you say to me,
how lucky I must be,
remember this melody;
It ain't easy being one.

SHORT STORIES

JACK AND DANIELLE
Reckless Love

I watched as Jack looked at the bottom of his empty glass to the whiskey-soaked ice cubes that seemed to call his pathetic name. As he blinked his hazel eyes, I saw how he prayed his tears were not as apparent as the gash on his right cheek. Licking his teeth, he asked me for another glass, somewhat hoping that the liquid poison would touch his lips one final time and everything would return to normal. I could see the desperation in his eyes. He sat there for a moment and looked at all the women in the bar, hoping to see Danielle's face one more time. She never did like it when he came home drunk.

As he kicked the mud from his boots, Jack took one more shot of tequila to finish the job. You see, I watched him sober up for two years, but those two years were wasted three months ago. She had always threatened him that if she caught him drinking again, she would ask him to leave for good, and he knew that she was right to do so. One time Jack told me that he knew he was violent when he drank. So, to me, Danielle was right to kick him out.

I glanced at him as he looked at the wood grain in the bar and took off his hat to relax into the night, drinking his cares away. It was as if everything in his world disappeared once he gulped down the goodness only whiskey could bring. I could see it in his cloudy eyes. That is, everything disappeared except for Danielle. She was like an immune subject for his alcoholic memory and Jack hated himself for it, I could tell.

After three more drinks, I decided to call a cab for Jack, only to see him disappear into the night before I could even pick up the phone. I had a sinking feeling in the pit of my stomach, so I looked for Jack's keys, but could not find them in the designated drawer. My heart sank as I watched him pull out of the parking lot and onto the highway. I wiped my hands on a towel and ran after the car, yelling for it to stop for the safety of not only Jack, but the rest of the road. I looked up at the Texas stars, knowing all I could do was call the police and wait for news about what had happened to him. I walked back into the bar and confiscated every key available to take, hoping that my mistake would be redeemed in some way. It was not until later that night, on the back of Jack's ticket, that I saw a feeble message written with ink and blurred by tears. The note read, "Till death do us part."

Jack was never my friend, but my heart ached when I saw this note, knowing it was for his wife, Danielle. Over the past month I had gotten to know about Jack, where he came from and how he got here. He would spend hours a day sitting in my bar drinking, but I could tell he was drinking to forget Danielle. I looked up from the glasses and saw an officer walk toward me with a flattened look on his face. When I heard Jack had died, I shed a few tears for him and asked how it happened. I was shocked to find out he was the only one in the accident that night. It seemed, he ran directly into a tree while going upwards of a hundred miles an hour. When I received this part of the news I told the officer what I knew of Jack and that he seemed fragile that night. It didn't strike me until then that I did not even know his last name.

The funeral was short and sweet with his brother, mother, and myself present. I assumed that since he spent his time drinking, Jack did not have many friends he could count on. I looked for the infamous Danielle, but she never showed her face. I assumed that she was right not to come, seeing that she was the ultimate cause of his death. I did not hear from his family again, but every time I saw a man drinking his heart away, I would stop and ask him for his first and last name. Sometimes, I would listen to their story and give advice, but most of the time they were too stubborn to hear what I had to say. Bar tending was a job I planned to have for a short amount of time, but I grew attached to it over the years. I hoped I could help the depressed see a way out of their darkness.

It was not until four years later that I came across a person as distraught as Jack was that night. I looked at the tears running down her pale white skin and saw what was left of her mascara on her cheeks. She had dark red hair and vivid green eyes, ones I had only heard described once. She looked at the wall behind me and laughed at the date circled on the wall. I looked at her and asked her what she wanted, but all she said was "whiskey" and returned to fixate on the date I circled four years ago. I looked at her clothes and gathered that she had come into the bar by chance, because she did not look like someone accustomed to drinking. She wore a nice dress and heels with a name-brand purse on the chair beside her, royally not blending into her surroundings. I asked her what her name was and she said that it did not matter, that what mattered was that she was no longer that girl anymore. She told me that she was tired of hiding at home and feasting on liquor in confidence like a child. I smiled at her as she remained fixed on the date. I looked at her and asked, "What is so interesting about that calendar?"

She looked at me as though I was an idiot sent from an evil abyss who had come to wreck her attempt at a good time. She ordered five glasses of whiskey and a shot of tequila, an order I recognized too well. I asked for her license and read the name "Danielle Martin" in bold black letters. My eyes grew wide and I looked at her and asked, "Did you know a Jack?"

With a gulp and a shot of tequila she answered, "Once."

My heart began to pound, knowing I had to save her for Jack's sake. She had the same look in her eyes that Jack had that night and I knew that she was troubled. She flashed me a smile and I felt like the only man in the room, a feeling I'm sure Jack felt at one point. Danielle held up her glass of whiskey and stated, "Four years ago I lost my husband to this drink. He was gone long before he was dead, but I drove him away both times."

I looked at her and tried to reason that Jack loved her even when she could not see the man she once knew, but she would not listen. I turned to pour another drink and heard the sounds of pills hitting the counter. As I turned I saw Danielle swallow seven times, washing each pill down with the drink that killed everything she hoped life would be. I gave her a look of despair, but she gave me a look of content as she flashed a picture before my eyes. I gazed at her in white, and Jack in black with a grin on his face. It was their wedding day. Danielle gave me an all-knowing smile as she folded the picture up and placed it in her purse. I watched as she walked out the door and into a cab. I had a feeling that she had just repeated history. However, all I could do was wait and see what lay ahead for Danielle Martin.

I turned on the news the next morning and saw a story of a woman who took too much of her own pain medication, but noted the picture they showed on the screen. The picture shown was of Danielle and Jack on their wedding day as the two shared a smile on the Galveston sand. The reporter said they found the picture next to the woman when they discovered her body. My breath felt cold as my diaphragm refused to work.

Danielle Martin's face was etched into my mind after that day and I dreamed of it every night. It was as if these two people loved each other so much that they both refused to live without one another, even if that meant death for themselves. It was almost like a modern twist to Romeo and Juliet.

When I went to Danielle's funeral, I stood in the back hoping that paying my respects would absolve me from the burden I carried. Danielle's crowd was much larger and aired on the side of hundreds, but I could not help but notice where her grave was placed. It had been four years since I had been at that gravesite, and I had hoped I would never return, but I had to go back. As I watched Danielle lay next to her husband, I felt an overwhelming peace inside me knowing that they were finally together as they should have been all along.

BURNING LOVE
Revengeful Love

Charleston, South Carolina 1855

It was a cold and dreary day when Ellie scraped up her paintings and began the long walk to town. Her face was tear stained and her demeanor was mournful as if she were mirroring the dark clouds above her. She wore a dark blue dress and carried her paintings in her arms. These paintings would never again be seen or admired. He had broken her heart and all she could think about was burning. Burning, burning the lies he had once spoken to her. In a brief moment she remembered his kind words. His eyes were once so full of trust, the most peaceful things she had ever seen, but now they had become dark portals to his wretched soul.

Ellie turned the corner and began to walk toward his home as the thought crossed her mind –Did she love him? Yes, but even so, things had become complicated after he became engaged to Jenna. Ellie felt the tears forming in her fragile eyes as she revisited the fact that he had chosen who he wanted and she was not the one he had chose. She passed by patrons on the street, hoping, wishing, and praying to see his face among the strangers. Ellie still had the faintest hope that he would return to her, even though she knew in her heart he was gone forever. She desired to see him over all things in her life, but forced herself to be disgusted by him so that she would have a reason to detest him. The hardest part for Ellie was that she loved him with everything she had. He had inspired every brush stroke on every canvas. All she wanted was to state her final opinion of him, extinguishing, not art, but the love in her heart that she knew would never die out on its own.

Ellie walked to the courtyard with the paintings in her hand as the morning mist rolled under her feet. The cold humid wind danced across her face as she turned a corner to see him sitting on a bench. Ellie felt as if she would vomit. He was sitting with a woman and showing something to her. Ellie's heart beat rapidly as she counted her paintings. The last one was missing. With a frantic breath and heavy heart she whispered, "No!"

She watched as Aaron put the canvas on the bench beside him. He rubbed his face with his hands, pondering a moment. Ellie saw the sweat pouring from his brow. He began to tell the woman that he could no longer marry her.

Ellie held her breath as Jenna looked at her fiancé with an understanding look of disappointment. The woman picked up Ellie's painting and replied, "When a man breaks an engagement it is either for money or because there is someone else. Please, tell me it is for money, Aaron."

Ellie moved in closer to hear their conversation, her stomach uneasy. She watched as he bowed his head and took Jenna's hands. "I am afraid I am in love with someone else. I do not wish to dishonor you in any way."

The woman stood up, fuming, and slapped him across the face. Something Ellie wished she had done months ago. The woman's eyes refused to look at Aaron as she curtsied, pulled off her ring, put it in his hand, and departed.

Ellie observed Aaron as he sat for a long while studying Ellie's painting of his garden. Something about seeing Aaron with the painting of what she dreamed their future to be, pulled on her heart. Tears fell, it was not a bellowing cry or a meek tear, but a heartfelt ache that Ellie had not been able to categorize for months. Her heart broke louder as each stroke was examined. Finally, Ellie could take no more. She took a small breath and stepped out of the shadows.

"Ellie, what are you doing here?"

She refrained from looking into his eyes and replied, "I

came back for what I left."

Aaron's eyes dimmed when he realize she meant her art. He handed it over to her slowly. "I am afraid I took it before you left."

Ellie looked in his eyes and with a cold edge in her voice replied, "You have taken so much of what is mine."

Aaron stood up and took the paintings from her. He placed them on the bench, inviting her to sit with him, but Ellie refused. He looked into her eyes and attempted to coerce her, "Ellie James, I am afraid you have what is mine." Ellie rolled her eyes, not willing to hear another pathetic excuse, but let him continue, "You are my every thought and you have my heart. I would never want to take from you what you have given to me freely. I was such a fool and I am truly sorry. One day I hope you can forgive me."

Ellie looked at her hands, pushing away the thought of her immanent love for him. She closed her eyes and reminded herself that he had robbed her of innocent love and tainted her belief in happy endings. She looked into the eyes of the man she once loved and retorted, "All I came here for was my painting. I see you have already shown it to Jenna."

"Jenna is gone. We are no longer engaged."

Ellie looked at Aaron as resentment boiled in her dark eyes, "Do you think that one sentence will make due for the agony I have received these past months? If you do think this, then you are mistaken and I can reasonably say that I have misjudged you as a man."

She began to walk away, but he took her hand. "Ellie, wait; How can I ever make up for my mistake?"

"Never make it again," she said as she snatched her painting from his hand, "but it looks as if you will not get that chance. Good day, sir."

Ellie closed her eyes as she turned away. She was grateful that her tears waited to fall until she was out of his sight. Ellie ran to the nearest field and the only thing that crossed her mind was, "Burning."

Aaron followed after her, curious to find where she was going. He recalled the anger in her eyes and knew what her intentions were. Ellie had always told him that inspiration was hard to find, but once it was tainted, the paintings would be worthless. The magnitude of his guilt peaked as he realized that he was her inspiration. Aaron ran after the woman he loved, hoping to save her from herself. Eventually, he came upon a short man with a white beard covered in ash. He panted for breath as he asked the man, "Sir, a woman passed by here; Where has she gone?"

The man looked at Aaron and pointed to a billow of smoke on top of the nearest hill. Panic ceased his voice as Aaron thanked the man. Memories of his and Ellie's friendship flashed before his eyes and Aaron found the answer to every question he had ever posed. Ellie was going to get rid of their memories once and for all.

Meanwhile, Ellie was standing before the glinting fire, sobbing. She recalled the tender moments and the pleasant times she had shared with Aaron. She looked at her paintings, her life's work. Should she toss them into the fire to be engulfed by the flames? Ellie closed her eyes as a tear fell on her left cheek. He did not love her. She glanced at her paintings once more and saw Aaron's face in her mind. Every emotion she had ever felt for him surfaced through her rage and despair. She began to scream, "I hate you. I hate you. I hate you!" Ellie put her paintings over the flames. She took a breath as she confessed, "I'll always love you."

She closed her eyes and let go of the paintings. A weight lifted from her shoulder. She felt free for the first time since she had met Aaron; however, when she looked down, she could not see her artwork in the fire. Ellie felt arms around her, clinging to the paintings, saving her from the regret she was destined to feel. The arms let go and Ellie turned to see to whom they belonged. She looked at Aaron intently, peering into his soul to find an answer as to why he followed her. Ellie stood silent as she stared at the man she was destined to love. She could not let Aaron win. Ellie felt hatred, envy, and love simultaneously as her eyes spilled tears that stung as they fell on her cheeks. As usual, Aaron said nothing.

"Why did you not let me do it?"

"I love you, Ellie."

Ellie studied his expression and the memory of the last three months whirled before her, but she only felt resentment toward him. "You, of all people, speak of love."

"Are you mocking me?"

"You mock me," she accused as she began to walk away from him. Ellie felt a hand on her back and heard Aaron's voice admit, "I came back for you, Ellie. Is that not what you want? All of the stories you read and love have happy endings. The rich man comes back and he and the female protagonist ride off together into the sunset."

Ellie rolled her eyes and turned to face Aaron, growing passionately against every inch of him. It was not that he loved her that made her so angry, but that he would come to her now after what he did.

"I did not want you to come back. I wanted you to never leave. Who are you to come back thinking I owe you a second chance? You are no one, and you will continue to be no one until the day you die. Only a child would do what you have done to me."

"Are you calling me a child?"

"You are certainly not a man. Did you think that I would consider you after what you have done? If you did, then you must be more naive than I ever imagined."

Aaron's expression cut into Ellie's soul and her heart began to break slower than before. She looked longingly into his eyes and thought of a life with Aaron. The idea was blissfully sweet, but she realized his eyes were no longer inviting, but cold. He had no soul. If he could humiliate her and break her heart once, he would do it again. She closed her eyes and let out a sigh, "That's just it. I do love you, but you took my most prized possession, my heart. You gave me inspiration and you showed me how to live, and for that I will always love you."

"Then, will you marry me, Ellie?"

Ellie saw the ring in his hand and felt sick to her stomach. She processed their conversation and realized that she would always love Aaron, but that she could never be in love with him, not after what he had done. Ellie took her paintings from Aaron and said, "No, Aaron. I am not a prize to be won or a damsel that needs to be rescued. Truthfully, if you had to come back for me, you never really loved me.

No man would leave the woman he loved for another, and because you did, I have a feeling you do not know what love is."

Aaron's mouth gaped open. His face looked broken, but Ellie walked past him as a smile crept across her lips. She was finally free. She turned around to look at him one last time to see the pain in his eyes and felt a sick and twisted pleasure from it. He now felt what she felt and revenge could not have tasted any sweeter.

A NIGHT TO REMEMBER
Forgotten Love

Lucy rounded the corner of the barricade feeling the various objects sticking out of the temporary wall. She looked to her right and saw three men lying dead on the cobblestone street she once called home. Lucy looked for her husband, but could not see his face among the lines of dead men. She took a breath and thanked God that he was not deceased. Night had always been Lucy's favorite, but this night was darker than all the others combined. Torches lit her way as she walked the perimeter of the barricade, searching for two familiar faces.

As Lucy turned around she saw the exact face she was hoping to find. She looked at the man and her hands began to shake as if the joy inside her was too strong for her body to absorb. Her legs moved toward him as he stood still with a blank expression on his face. Lucy touched his mud-caked face as if he were a lost child newly found. "Richard?"

He gave her a blank look as he replied, "You should not be here."

Lucy's eyebrows came together. "I came here for you and for my brother. You two are too important to me to be lost forever in this street."

"You must believe that I know what is best for you. We deserve freedom, Lucy."

"What is freedom without the ones you love?" she questioned as she shook her head in disbelief.

Lucy looked up at the stars in the sky and then back to

her husband. He had always had a bright spirit, but the uprising had taken its toll on him as it had every other man in France who desired freedom. She rubbed her eye to rid it of a tear and then pushed back her light blonde hair. "I cannot think of you getting hurt."

Richard looked at her with the tenderness Lucy had desperately longed to see. She swallowed and asked, "Will you leave tomorrow with me and my brother?"

"Michael has agreed to leave?"

She lifted up her eyelids and replied, "Not yet."

A loud noise came from the left as Lucy shot up and outward. With a crack the barricade began to fall and Richard joined her on the ground. The thumping of her head was like a beating drum that drowned out the cries of injured men. Lucy looked at her husband, who was not awake, and a tear fell from her eye. She blinked it back and looked beyond him to the men who lay on the ground, injured and screaming. Red was all she saw and blood was all she smelled. Lucy tried to sit up and wake Richard, but her arm could not support her weight. Turning to her other side, she began to crawl by placing her right elbow on the ground. Lucy became dizzy, but took a breath and steadied her balance as she crawled to find help.

Men turned and looked at her as if she were a ghost, but Lucy kept on searching for help and her brother, knowing he was most likely close to the action. As she stumbled upon injured men she aided them as much as she could, but her efforts were in vain for the most part. She tended to one man's shoulder and another's leg, but in a matter of seconds they had no blood left in their frail and beaten bodies. Lucy crawled to the next victim and tied his arm off, but his eyes rolled back in his head before she could finish the knot. Lucy let out a sigh and put her face to the cold cobblestone. Her emotions had not yet caught up to her present circumstance, but Lucy knew that it was for the best. She closed her hazel eyes and lay on the ground for a moment. Streams of blood and mud hit the side of her face as they trickled against the stone street. Her mouth tasted like copper, but Lucy coughed up some of the blood and swallowed the rest as she crawled back to her husband. She reached his side in time to shake him awake. Richard gasped for air that would not come, but when it finally reached his lungs, a smile slid onto her face.

"How long has it been?"

"Not long," she said as she rested her head on the ground. Lucy closed her eyes as if she was searching for strength to stay alive. She licked her chapped lips and cleared her throat as she uttered, "We should have left."

"You should not have come," Richard said as he took his wife's hand.

Smiles were all Lucy had left and she desired to share them with Richard. "We are having a child, Richard."

"A baby?"

Lucy nodded as she watched him grab his stomach. His shirt was turning red, but Lucy refused to believe Richard would leave her. She looked at her blood-soaked hands and back to his amiable expression. With a whisper Richard reminded her, "I love you."

"I love you too," she said as she watched her husband close his eyes. Lucy was numb, she took a breath as Richard became a blurred image. Then, darkness.

The pressure on Lucy's chest woke her from her dreams. As she opened her eyes, she saw another set looking back at her. The woman before her was quite plump and had a welcoming smile and warm cheeks. Lucy's fingers felt the blanket under her and felt that her head was cushioned by a pillow. Her eyes widened as she looked at the woman. "Where am I?"

"You are in a hospital in London, Mrs."

Lucy turned her head to look for Richard, but could only see the pale wallpaper on the bland blue wall. She looked at the woman and asked, "Where is my husband?"

"Did you go back again, Mrs.?", the woman asked as she handed her a cup of water.

Lucy shook her head up and down as the woman held her up so she could sip the water. Lucy smiled at the woman and thanked her for the drink. She felt her legs, which she noted had shrunk substantially in size. Her hair was tucked behind her head, but was much thinner than she recalled. Lucy sipped the water, hoping that by making herself well,

Richard would appear.

A man and a woman entered the door with two children, but Lucy paid them no attention. The plump woman smiled kindly as she introduced the four people, "Mrs, this is Elizabeth, Matthew, Lucy and Steven."

Lucy looked at the little girl who shared her name and smiled. She looked up at the plump woman, who seemed to be some sort of caregiver, and inquired as to why they were in her room. The woman touched her shoulder and did not reply. Lucy pushed the question from her mind and welcomed the new company. She looked at the younger woman and asked, "Are these your children?"

The woman replied with a faint yes as she slid her husband a glance. Lucy was disturbed by the woman's apathetic expression. "Where is Richard?"

The man came toward her and took her hand. She gave him a look of confusion as the man answered, "He is not coming."

"Richard will come. Richard always comes."

"No."

"Yes."

"No."

Lucy's face turned red as she raised her voice, "Richard will not leave me here!"

The man put his hand to his face as if he was the messenger of poor news. Lucy leaned closer to him and shook her head awaiting his reply.

The man, Matthew, had a faint darkness in his expression and a hint of sorrow in his voice. He took off his hat and placed it on the table beside Lucy's bed. He gave Lucy a piece of clear metal in which she saw wrinkles on her face and gray in her hair. "Richard is dead, Mother."

COFFEE
Envious Love

It was October 27 and the streets of New York City were cold and crowded. Before you begin this story, you must know that this is not a romance and it is not an adventure; It is a story of life. A story that started with coffee.

Sarah walked out of the train station and into the street. Her heart was racing and her hands were shaking. She tucked her train ticket into her jacket pocket and took a breath. She had made it to the Big Apple; the best place on earth. It was a dream come true. She was from a small town where the ratio of cows to humans was particularly unbalanced. Sarah, being new to the city, decided that she needed to try a cup of coffee. It was not that they did not have coffee in her town, it was just that it tasted like the beans had not been crushed properly. Sarah peeled off into the first coffee shop she saw and waited in a line that seemed to go on for ages. The people around her were very diverse and she felt as if they were all speaking a different language.

When she got to the front of the line, she was lost in the immense variations of caffeine and expresso. With no coffee dictionary at hand, she settled for black. While waiting for her rather tasteless coffee, she sat at a table for two and watched the busy street before her. Her name was called and she retrieved the cup. The second she tasted the bitter drink, she spit it out of her mouth. It was almost like she licked a monkey's armpit. Sarah was disgusted by what happened, and looked up to see a man who seemed to get a kick out of it.

She approached the man with her coffee and commented, "Excuse me, sir, but I was raised knowing that pointing and laughing at people is rude. So, if you could refrain from laughter, that would be great."

"My name is Corey Keller."

He stuck out his hand and she reluctantly shook it. Sarah looked at the man. She smiled slightly because the man was actually quite attractive.

"Well, Corey Keller, I am Sarah," She looked at him closely and added, "You seem awfully familiar."

"Where are you from?"

"Davis. It is a small town in Iowa."

"Sarah Barker? It's Corey Keller, I went to high school with you."

Sarah's heart jumped and heat came to her cheeks. Why had she not recognized him? "Corey!"

"Yes! I cannot believe it! It has been so long."

"Seven years, I'm afraid," she said with an awkward smile.

"The odds of running into you in the city, apparently they are good," he replied with a grin Sarah knew all too well.

He looked at her for a while and she saw him glance at his watch. "I'm late."

"What are you late for?"

"I have a meeting with a photographer," he squinted as he tilted his head to the left. "Why do you ask?"

"It was just good to see an old friend so soon in this city."

"I am meeting my fiance at the photographer's, but I know she would love to meet you."

Sarah's eyes widened, not knowing her old crush had popped the question to a random woman from New York. "Well, I would love to meet her," she lied as she gave him her number, "Just contact me later."

He gave a polite smile as he ducked out of the coffee shop.

Sarah watched as he left, not knowing what to feel. Where they were from, the high school football star and head cheerleader always ended up together and produced the next generation of athletes. Of course, Corey had to go off to the big city and defy tradition. Sarah rolled back her eyes and sipped the bitter coffee in her cup. The coffee was terrible, but too expensive to give away to a stranger and definitely too pricey to be trashed. So, Sarah forced herself to drink it as she watched the people on the street.

There were so many people in the street that one could people watch for days. Sarah was captivated by the many different shapes and sizes of the people. The woman across the room was staring at Sarah, making her feel even more uncomfortable in this new city. She picked up her cup and walked over to the woman. "What?"

The woman wore leather and chains, opposite Sarah's sun dress and heels. She shot Sarah a terrifying glance and then broke into a small smile. "Jerk?"

"Excuse me?"

The woman leaned on the table and asked, "Was he a jerk?"

Sarah gathered she was talking about Corey and replied, "Oh no, that was just an old friend I just found out is now engaged, actually."

The woman curled her lip and took a sip of her green looking goop. I've seen him around here. I work the later shift and he comes in after work sometimes.

Sarah looked at the woman and squinted, "Have you seen his fiance?"

"Yeah," she lifted her eyebrow and leaned closer to Sarah, "Jealous?"

"No, I don't think so."

"You should get back at him," the woman said with a smirk on her black painted lips.

Sarah smiled with her pink ones and replied, "I don't think that would be a good idea."

"Why not?"

"Corey was a great friend, we dated for seven years. I could not do anything to hurt him."

"What if you just hurt her?"

Sarah pointed to the seat across from the woman asking if she could sit with her. The woman shook her head and Sarah took a seat as she folded her cherry-printed dress under herself. "How exactly would that happen?"

"Well, I know she's allergic to peanuts. Always reminding me that she is special in that way."

"What exactly does she look like?"

The woman gave out a loud brutal laugh, "Basically like you."

"Like me?"

"Except she has green eyes and she's a little shorter. Anyways, I know what we can do."

Sarah looked at her new friend's piercings and gathered that this had not been her first attempt at scheming. "What?"

"I can slip some peanuts into her big blend of calories, she'll never notice."

"Will it hurt her?"

"Just enough for a scare," the woman said as she took another sip from her green goop.

Sarah pondered what she should do, but as she thought her phone went off. She looked at the woman and answered it. Corey wanted to meet in an hour at the same coffee shop. It was almost as if it was meant to be. Sarah looked at the woman and replied, "Let's do it."

An hour later Corey walked into the coffee shop with a woman that looked much like Sarah. Sarah nodded to her new friend, who was now working, that they had arrived. The two love birds ordered and came to sit with Sarah.

Sarah stood to her feet and shook hands with her friend and his fiance. As they sat down they began by saying things happy couples normally say and describing in detail how they met. It seems as if their love had blossomed so quickly it only took them a month to know that they were destined to be together. It sounded like crap to Sarah. It was not too long into the conversation that Dianna, Corey's fiance, began to clear her throat. She smiled and blamed it on her vocal career. However, when she could no longer breathe there was no career to blame. She slammed her hand on the table as her eyes opened wide. She took Corey by the arm as he called an ambulance. He poked her with a shot thing, but even that was not enough. Sarah's hands began to sweat when she realized that Dianna was slowly dying. She tried to help by trying to keep Dianna calm, but all her attempts failed, except her initial one. Corey looked disoriented and confused when the medic called her time of death. Sarah looked at the woman behind the bar and began to shake her head. The woman smiled as she shrugged and whispered, "Oops."

Corey stood still as they carried off his fiance. Sarah attempted to comfort him, but he refused to let her touch him. He looked at her with brokenness in his once tender eyes and said he was sorry, but he had to go make some calls. Sarah could not stand the feeling of guilt that now rested upon her shoulders. She looked at Corey and picked up her coffee cup as she said, "I think I better go."

"I think you should."

As Sarah left the coffee shop she took one last swig of her bitter drink before she trashed it for good. New York was supposed to be a new adventure, but all it did was leave Sarah back where she began.

VRIEND
Misunderstood Love

Day 1,

They're gone now. Good. I thought they would never leave. I love this bus stop. It's probably the most fantastical place in the world. Girls and boys of all ages waiting to learn or coming back from learning. I would like to learn. Mamma never did let me learn, but Daddy did teach me lessons. Most involved a belt or the back of his hand, but that's okay, because he loved me. They both did. Mamma said so. I like watching the children. They are wonders to me, so happy and so juvenile. They are like fresh fallen snow, pure and white. I put down my coffee and folded my paper to leave, like I did every day, but today was different. As I rounded the corner in my van I saw her for the first time. She was beautiful. I shook my head, knowing that people would find me strange for liking a six-year-old girl when I was forty-three, but we were friends. I would make sure we were friends. We had to be friends. I need friends.

Day 4,

Work was boring today. Work is always boring, because fast food is not really all that fast on Tuesdays anyway. I like my job, but I most like watching the fries boil in the grease. It is calming. Mamma used to boil potatoes every sunday after church. I hated mass, because it was all in a different language, but Mamma wouldn't let me skip. She said grandpa and grandma never let her skip. I never met them, but she said they were nice. I think they still live in Holland.

That's where Mamma is from. "Vrienden, Horace. Je vrienden nodig hebt," she would always say. I never knew what that meant until I found the internet and searched for it. She was just saying that I needed friends. "Friends, Horace. You need friends." I had my friends in my mind, but Mamma said I needed real ones. That's okay though, because I have one friend now. I don't know her name, but I know we could be friends. She seems nice. Maybe I'll introduce myself after she gets home from school.

Day 10,
    I said "hi" to her today. She was wearing the cutest little skirt and had pigtails in her hair. I like her hair in pigtails. It is strange to me that we have never met before. Maybe after school one day we could go to the park or something. Mamma always said that it was nice to go places with friends and to do fun things. Well, I like the park. If I could, I would take her to the park after school, but her Mamma always comes to pick her up at the bus stop. It's a shame, really. I think we could be great friends.

Day 11,
    Today I brought her some ice cream. Now she knows my name and my face and I can talk to her and she'll reply. People keep giving me strange looks when I talk to her, but we are only friends and I would never hurt her. Why do people think I would want to hurt her? She likes her teddy bear most of all, she says, but I think she likes her doll the most, because I see her playing with it through her window. Sometimes I sit and watch her, but not too often, because people start to ask me why I'm there and I know they would not understand. I think I love her.

Day 13,
    I don't know what to do. I was talking to her like I always do, but then her Mamma walked out of the house to come and get her so I asked her to get in the car with me. I just wanted to talk to her more. I saw her Mamma panic when she was not at the bus stop, so I drove away so she would not yell at me. I hate it when people yell at me.

Day 14,

She's been asking for her Mamma, but I told her we would meet mine soon. She cries a lot, but I gave her some more ice cream and she stopped. I even got her a doll that looked like the one she played with in her room. I hope she likes it. She started to bang on the windows of my van, so I had to tie her up. I didn't want to, but I had to so she would not hurt herself. I think she is scared and I wish she wasn't because I just want her to be my friend. I told her I would take care of her but she just looked down and cried even more. She's so pretty, even when she cries.

Day 15,

I was watching TV today and I saw her face on the screen next to mine. I think they know I have her, but they can't take her yet, because we haven't even gone to the park. Mamma said that friends go to the park together, and we are friends. We have to go to the park.

Day 16,

Today was a sad day. They asked me a lot of questions and even searched my room. Good thing they did not look in my van. I left it at work so they would not ask about it. Mamma told them to leave because I would never take an innocent girl from her family. Mamma doesn't know. I just wanted a friend like she always said I needed. I have one now. Mamma doesn't even believe that I would have a friend as pretty or "adorable" as her. If Daddy was here now he'd just assume I took her for no good reason, but Mamma always saw the good in me. When the dog died Daddy blamed me, but Mamma knew I just wanted a friend and held her too tight. I loved my dog. When I saw his eyes change I knew he was finally happy. That's all I want, to make people happy.

Day 17,

They took her away today. Her Mamma and Daddy were so happy to see her and she was happy to see them. They gave her the teddy bear, but I know she liked her doll better! I loved her and I know she loved me. Mamma shook her head when she saw me going away with the police. I thought Mamma would have been happy I found a friend. Now I'm all alone and I don't know when I'll see Mamma again. When her Daddy carried her away she looked back at me and I got to see her face one last time before I rolled away. She waived to me. She said goodbye in that moment and right then I knew she really was my friend. Mijn vriend.

THE STATION
Idealistic Love

Charles Young combed back his black hair as he looked in the mirror to see himself in uniform for the first time. His tan clothes contrasted against his pale white face. While touching his buttons his fingers grew cold, partly because of the chill of the buttons themselves, but mostly because the thought of war disturbed him. Charles had never been a man to fight, but since the cause was so great, he could think of no greater honor. He rubbed his hands over his oiled hair and placed his cap on his head. With a breath he opened the door to exit the bathroom. As he turned to grab his things he saw his wife and son waiting to say their farewells.

Charles crossed the room to his wife, Shirley, and son, Walter. Kneeling to the ground, he embraced his son before he said his goodbyes. Charles' heart broke when his son refused to let go, but knew that by going to fight, his son would have a reason to be proud of his father. Charles only hoped that Walter would follow in his ways and stand against oppressors of the innocent. The boy began to cry, but Charles suggested that England was not too far away and that he would be back very soon.

Shirley's sorrowful glance caught his attention and Charles stood to his feet. "I will not be gone long. After I return, we will live in peace. I am sure Hitler and his men will give in sooner than later."

"You are a good man, Charlie, and I love you for it," she replied as she fixed his tie.

Charles wiped a tear from her cheek. "I will come home safe, I promise. I will always come back for you two."

Shirley and Charles shared a kiss as he picked up a single bag. He was glad that his family was not coming to the station, because Charles did not want that to be Walter's last memory of his father.

The walk to the station was nothing but agonizing for Charles. All the while he questioned whether he was doing what was right in his family's eyes, but most importantly in God's. Charles felt a sense of obligation to the men and women, of his own race and faith, that were being persecuted in Germany, but he also felt an obligation to Shirley and Walter. Arriving at the station, he set eyes on his friend, Larry.

Larry was strange and of shorter height, but nonetheless a good man and Charles' best friend. He and Larry had worked together for years at the local mechanics shop in their small rundown town in Tennessee. Charles greeted his friend with a solid hand shake and pat on the back.

***

Three years had passed since Charles left and Shirley Young was slowly coming undone. She looked at herself in the mirror and saw the ever present circles under her eyes. Shirley looked at Charles' picture as she let out a sigh of regret, knowing he was dead. She slammed her hands against the wall, only to startle her son in the adjacent room. She felt a panic surge through her as she reached for the lock on the bathroom door. "Mother, are you alright?" she heard her son call from beyond the door that served as a barrier. Tears fell on her blouse as she sniffled and wiped her nose. "Mother is just a little tired today, Walter."

Shirley turned her attention back to the old family portrait in her shaking pale hand. Charles. He was dead and she was sure. With no word from him in three years after the millions of letters sent, there was no other explanation.

Shirley wiped the salt water off her face and powdered her fair skin with frail hands. Placing the photograph back in her pocket she opened the door to see her son standing before her in his best shirt. "Will father be there today?"

Shirley smiled at her son and tucked his cotton shirt into his breeches. Fixing a stray piece of hair on his head, she replied, "We shall see."

The train station was like a gas chamber for Shirley and Walter was it's only optimism. She felt him clench her hand as they waited for the train of men to arrive. Women with watery eyes and children with smiles waited to see who would step off the train, and they all hoped it would be their loved one. With a screeching stop the train arrived and the women held their breath, but Shirley was not so hopeful. She had been here what seemed like thousands of times, and each time she held her breath, but this time was different. There was no use looking for Charles.

Women lit up when they saw their men and some collapsed when they received a flag as a replacement. Shirley waited until the station was empty and then turned to Walter only to see his small smile. They walked home disappointed, but Shirley had a feeling that something was not quite right. She saw a woman pass her with a toddler on her hip. "The train has already left."

The woman looked at her with bright blue eyes and replied, "There is another train. I heard it coming this way."

"That is not possible. There is always only one train."

"Not today Ms., there is also a train of men sent from France," the young girl said as she repositioned her child.

Shirley looked down at her hopeful son and replied, "Well, it certainly could not hurt to check."

The woman gave her another smile as she tucked her disheveled blonde hair behind her ears. She looked to be nineteen years of age and her child seemed to be two years old. Shirley studied the young hopeful woman and asked, "Who are you waiting for?"

"My husband," she said as they climbed the brown steps. "And you?"

"Same," Shirley replied with mournful eyes.

"He will come, Ms."

"You seem so sure."

"My Danny said to me that he would come back and I believe him. He has to, you see. Little Bethany and I need him just as you and your son need your husband."

"What if he doesn't come back?'

"I will not think of that until it becomes reality," the woman said as she placed her daughter on the floor.

In the distance, a train rolled down the track and Shirley's heart began to beat faster as if the world was about to stop. As the train doors opened she saw many faces, but could not see Charles and immediately felt ashamed for even thinking he was on the train.

She heard the woman next to her call out her husband's name as he stepped off the train. Watching a father meet his daughter for the first time was always something Shirley enjoyed, but when she saw a flag coming toward her, her knees went weak. The red, white, and blue faded into a color that repulsed her. She held her breath as Walter grasped her leg. The man asked, "Are you Mrs. Charles Young?"

Should she lie? If she did not reveal that she was the deceased's wife, could she live on pretending he was alive? No. She have to be brave for her son. Walter needed an answer. She needed an answer. "Yes, Sir."

The man looked over his shoulder and called, "Charlie, she's over here!"

Shirley looked past the man before her and saw the familiar face she dreamed of nightly. Her breath was gone and she stood frozen in a moment of incandescent joy. Walter called for his father as he ran into his arms, soaking his father's uniform with cheerful tears. Shirley moved slowly toward her husband, not able to utter a sound. She looked into her husband's eyes as she cherished her son's faint cries, hoping she was not dreaming. Charles touched her chin and commented, "I told you, I will always come back for you, Shirley."

CRYSTAL BETH ROBINSON
Addictive Love

Crystal Beth Robinson was George's everything. It was as if she was a part of him that would never cease to exist. Crystal was like a pleasurable cancer stuck to him for the remainder of eternity. George would have given anything he had to stay with Crystal. He knew the five stages of grief, he had experienced them all, but Crystal and his separation was only to appease others, not to please himself. George would always remember the sigh of relief his mother gave when he agreed to quit her once and for all.

He looked at the sunset as it reflected on the ocean, but in this peaceful scene he wished for Crystal. She was a part of him, a part he knew he could not live without. As the salty ocean breeze graced his face, George walked onto the white sand. His dress shoes filled with hot sand that felt like warm oatmeal on his aching feet. Beaches brought a comfort to George that he could never comprehend. Maybe it was the way the waves fell on the sand or the salt in the breezy air. Nonetheless, it was a place of serenity where he first laid eyes on her.

As George breathed in, his lungs rejected the air. They only wanted to inhale Crystal's scent. He heard footsteps from behind and assumed that his brother was babysitting him once again. Johnny had been watching over him since the breakup which was a bittersweet idea for George. He had not seen his friends since the initial breakup and did not wish to see them until he was strong enough to have moved past Crystal. So, Johnny's presence was a comfort for

George. George might have left her on his own, but instead, his family had taken her away from him. He loved his family, but he loved her too; how could they make him choose?

As the streets of Los Angeles began to crowd for the night, he walked down the sidewalk hoping to find some trace of her. He remembered that she loved this beach when the sun was down and the moon was out. It was her time of night. George could remember how their relationship first started, and how he would sneak down to the beach and meet with her. They would sit and talk with one another, but George knew even then that he would never be able to get enough time with her. Pulling his imagination back to reality, George rounded the corner to their usual spot beneath the pier, but he saw his brother's face instead of the woman he loved. Just beyond Johnny, George could see Crystal with his former friends and longed to engage in their conversation, but Johnny took George by the shoulder. George felt ashamed when Johnny looked at him as if he had seen the burial of a beloved family member. George looked back into his brother's sympathetic eyes and confessed, "I've tried to forget her, Johnny, I have."

"You will in time," Johnny replied as he led George up the beach and onto the street. Johnny helped his brother back onto the road and could see that George had talked with Crystal since the last time they were together.

George looked back at Crystal as they walked away and saw that the beauty in her had not faded over the past few months. Their separation had been sudden and without warning, but George's family believed it was for the best. George hoped he would eventually feel the same. However, that did not mean George would ever forget Miss Robinson or the effect she had on him. Every time she touched him it was as if he had reached heaven for the first time. His head would spin and his senses would be heightened by her irrevocable beauty. George could not let her go. He would not let her go.

As they came to his parent's home, George thanked his brother and walked through the door, hoping his parents were not home. However, he was hit with the sweet aroma of apple pie and gingerbread, a scent that once brought comfort to him. Now, the holidays were the worst for George, because he had to be with the people who forced him out of what he thought was a perfect relationship. His mother was his only comfort during the breakup; she understood what it was like to let go of someone. His mother had been with a man while she was married to George's father, but George now knew that his mother loved the other man more than she could ever love his father. It was exactly how he felt about his precious Crystal, she would always come first. George looked at his red-headed aging mother and forced a smile on his cracked lips and watched as she gave him a compassionate grin. "Christmas dinner will be ready shortly, dear. Your sister and brothers will be here soon, so straighten up and fix the table."

George let out a mumble that evolved into a painful wail. He clenched his stomach as he felt the ever present desire for Crystal rise to it's full potential. His mother rounded the kitchen corner to take his hand, but when she saw her husband she turned to leave the room. George's father poked him with his cane, disgusted that he had raised such a weak human. "Be a man George and set the table like your mother said."

Tears flowed from George's eyes, "No!"

"Suit yourself," his father replied with a stern look as he left the room to console his grieving wife.

George rubbed his forehead and fiddled with his hands as if he was wringing water out of a towel. He reluctantly set the table and watched as his mother re-entered the room with tears on her cheeks. George saw the way his mother looked at him and how ashamed his father felt to have raised him as a son. George knew what he had to do, but was not pleased with himself after he had come to the conclusion to do it. However, he knew it had to be done. George did not want to hurt his mother, but he had to have Crystal. He took the knife out of his pocket and placed it on his neck. "Give me money or I'll cut."

His mother's forced sweet complexion turned sour as she pleaded, "George do not be foolish."

"I'll do it."

His mother dug in her purse for spare cash, but his father put his tender shaking hand over his wife's. "Then do it son."

"Randall," his mother retorted in astonishment.

"Father!"

"Be a man, George. This entire family is better without her. You have seen the way your nieces and nephews look at you when she is around. She is not good for you, George."

"I love her Dad. I love her more than you seem to love me," he replied as he approached the elderly couple. He looked into his mother's warm and loving eyes as he snatched the money from her trembling hand.

George slammed the door and walked back to the spot Crystal called home. With shaking hands he planned out what he would say to her father when he asked to see Crystal. With money to repay the cash he owed her father, George was sure he would forgive him and give Crystal back to him. As he approached the pier, sweat formed on his brow, but George knew that a woman like Crystal was worth everything he had, even if his family did not approve. It was as if she had cast a spell on him, a spell he was incapable of escaping –A spell he did not wish to be freed from.

When he reached the spot under the pier, George strung together a few small sentences through his stammering that was enough to get his request across. He looked at the man before him who was tall and had a bone–chilling essence about him. George then looked to Crystal who stood behind the man. She looked better than he remembered and smelled sweeter than he could have imagined. The man shoved her forward, giving her to George for the first time in months. He stared at her beauty and thanked the man, her father, for understanding their relationship and his parent's judgement. Crystal seemed to be happy with him, and George knew he was in heaven with her by his side.

George walked into his mother's house as the family gathered around the table for supper. Heads turned toward him and a hot feeling of regret slapped his cheeks. His brother shook his head when he saw Crystal as he instructed the women and children to leave the room, just like they had at Thanksgiving the previous year. George saw no problem with the woman he wanted to spend the rest of his life with, but it seemed his family could not get over the fact that he loved this woman with his everything. His soul was bare without her and every single one of his family members knew that kicking Crystal out of his life would be like forcing oxygen out of his lungs.

"Get out," his father said with a furrowed brow.

George looked to his mother for support, but only saw a weary expression. His father continued, "We do not want her here George."

George turned to his girlfriend and looked into her inviting eyes. She tasted as sweet as he had remembered. His head began to spin as he saw his family clearly for the first time that day. Johnny took Crystal by the arm and shoved her out of the home, locking the door to keep her out once and for all. Nonetheless, George felt no pain as he fell to the ground, hoping he could have Crystal one more time.

Johnny looked at George, who laid on the floor numb to the touch. "What do you need, George?"

"I love her, Johnny."

"You can't love her, George, she will kill you."

"Freedom. Then, I want freedom from her."

Johnny smiled at his little brother and helped him to the couch where he would stay for the night. Johnny looked in George's pants pocket and saw four pictures of Crystal. He looked at the photographs and then back to his brother. Johnny took the pictures and showed them to his father. They both walked into the bathroom with the photos and decided the best way for George to forget about Crystal was to rid her from his memory. They lifted the polished white lid of their household toilet and flushed away the pictures that George held so highly in his heart.

While his family was disposing of what they believed was George's only tie to Crystal, George took from his other pocket his last picture of Crystal. As he looked at it, he realized that what his family thought meant nothing to him. While his family was concerned with how people looked at them, all he wanted was for them to look at him and see that he needed more help than he initially believed. He would always have Crystal and he would always keep her. George kissed the picture as his family entered the room. George's heart began to beat fast and his palms began to sweat as his mother dialed for the ambulance. Johnny pleaded with George to not close his eyes. However, George disobeyed his brother's demands and closed his eyes to take in the sweet embrace of his beloved.

***

As Johnny watched his brother leave his parent's home in a body bag, he contemplated why his brother would betray them in this way. His heart ached at the sight of his mother's tears and his brother's deceased body, but this image would forever be ingrained into his mind. George had known the hold methamphetamines had on their family, but still chose to partake in them. Johnny looked behind the bushes and saw the bag of crystal meth he had thrown out of the home hours before the coroner arrived. When he picked up the drugs he shook his head as if by hoping tonight had never happened, he could ease the pain in his stomach. Johnny looked to his father and they both agreed that Crystal would have to be taken care of just as she had in the past.

FIRST LOVE LOST
Unrequited Love

New Orleans, 1925

Isabella Archer made her way down the lively streets of New Orleans with youth in her heart and a swing in her step. She wore a loose-fitting green dress with fringe down the front and back. Her black gloves graced her delicate hands and her natural red smile lined her white teeth. She looked to her left and saw her childhood friend, Irene Matthews, and Irene's older brother Lucas. Isabella walked toward them through the crowded street and commented on Irene's black dress and feather. The cobblestone under her feet were unstable, but she refused Lucas' free arm to steady her weight. He laughed at her with his green eyes as Isabella looked at him and commented, "I see you dolled up for this occasion, Lucas."

He gave her a quick smile and then elbowed his sister, "You know I spend hours getting ready for outings such as these."

"Oh, hush. No one wants to hear you beat your gums," Irene said with a distinct look in her hazel eyes.

Isabella blushed on Lucas' behalf and replied, "I do not suppose your brother revels in spending his nights with us dames."

"I rather enjoy it actually," he said with a boyish grin on his smooth face. Isabella noticed small lines on his forehead and came to realize that the small boy she once knew had aged. Isabella felt her own skin and was relieved it was still as tight as it was the day she was born. Being twenty-seven, Isabella knew her time to age was coming soon, but she was not as fixated on it as Irene. Irene used creams and herbs to keep her youth, even though she was only one year Isabella's senior. They passed an unstable man who had illegal liquor in the bag from which he drank. Isabella was disgusted that a man would drink to the point that he could no longer stand. The streets smelled of vomit and urine thanks to men who loved their bourbon more than their lives. She scrunched her nose and Lucas commented, "Charming isn't it?"

She rolled her eyes and Irene let out a loud laugh as she always did. They walked up to the party and smooth jazz music filled the air. The sound of the saxophone was carried by the wind and enchanted Isabella from the moment it touched her ears. They walked into the joint and saw many people dancing to the revolutionary music. Isabella engaged in some static conversation, but was quickly unimpressed and ready to leave. However, Irene encouraged her to stay a while and enjoy the music. Lucas excused himself to talk with a buddy from the university. Isabella looked around the room, but her eyes followed Lucas. He was thirty years old, but looked as If he was still in his twenties. He was a reputable man and a great brother to Irene. Isabella looked to her right and saw that Irene was no longer there and searched the room for her, only to see her dancing with a decent-looking man. Isabella smiled at her friend and enjoyed the music that Irene begged her to stay and hear. Weary from the walk, Isabella found a seat in the corner of the room and sat to take in the sights and sounds. She finished her tea and licked her lips, satisfied that she was no longer thirsty. She looked around the room for her friends and saw that they were having a wonderful time. Isabella turned when she felt a man staring at her profile from the left. He wore a dark grey suit, a maroon tie and held a hat in his hand. His jawline was defined and his brown hair fell across his forehead. He smiled at her and Isabella felt her heart race as she gave him a polite smile. He gestured to the seat next to her. "May I take a seat here, Miss?"

She looked at his friendly smile and replied, "I suppose it wouldn't hurt."

He took a seat and the two sat awkwardly for a while, but Isabella decided to focus on the music and not the stranger to her left. He was rather attractive and he did not look to be a schemer or bootlegger. However, there was something mysterious about him, because in all her time in New Orleans she had never seen him. Isabella laughed at herself for thinking this, because New Orleans was a large city and there was no possible way she knew everyone who had ever entered it. She could tell the man heard her small giggle and her face blushed. He moved closer to her and asked, "May I ask what you are laughing at?"

"Myself, I'm afraid," she said with a small grin on her red lips. Isabella turned back to listen to the music, but she felt his eyes on her and turned to ask, "What is your name?"

"I thought you would never ask. My name is Raymond Dailey. What is your name?"

Isabella was enchanted by his kindness and willingness to approach her. She fixed a small piece of hair on her head and replied, "Isabella Archer. What brings you here?"

"Some old friends from my school days. I am sure you know some of them."

"You're so sure, but you have never met me," she said with a roll of her eyes.

Raymond laughed and replied, "I only guess so, because this is a reunion celebration after all."

Isabella threw back her head and put her hand to her chest as if she had no idea that the party was for Lucas' graduation reunion. She gasped melodramatically and flirted, "I had no idea that this was a closed party. How foolish of me!"

She saw Raymond's eyes brighten as dimples formed on his cheeks. "You are a very bold woman, Isabella Archer."

"I hope that is not a problem for you, Raymond Dailey."

"I rather like a woman who is bold enough to speak her mind," he said as he sat closer to her.

Isabella felt her stomach flitter and her cheeks blush once more. "Who did you come with?" she asked as she tucked a black curl behind her head.

"I came with myself. The question is who you came with, because I assume you are not always alone like you are tonight."

Isabella pointed to Lucas and replied, "I am here with Lucas Matthews and his sister. Do you know him?"

Raymond tilted his head and Isabella watched as he studied Lucas. He shrugged his shoulders and answered, "I suppose I saw him and we were friends once, but I do not remember him well."

Isabella watched Lucas dance with Irene and smiled. She could sense that Raymond believed they were going together, so she commented, "We have been friends since childhood and were raised as brother and sister."

Isabella turned to see Raymond's eyebrow lift. He put his arm around her and looked into her eyes. She internally pleaded for Lucas to come over and ruin the moment, but at the same time, she did not want the moment to end. Isabella looked down and Raymond kissed her cheek. Isabella was shocked by his actions and retreated. She saw that he was offended by her action and replied, "I was not expecting that."

"Neither was I," he said with a blush on his cheeks, "I would like to see you again, Isabella."

"I would like that too," she said with a grin on her lips.

"Very well. Shall we meet here tomorrow night?"

Isabella shook her head and Raymond took her hand. Feeling a bit warm, Isabella looked up to watch Lucas and Irene, but found that Lucas was already looking at her. The look on his face was one she had never seen before. It was a look of despair and hatred mixed with joy and sorrow, and when their eyes met, Isabella saw Lucas put down his drink and walk over to them. Within ten seconds Lucas was standing before her and Raymond.

Lucas looked at Isabella as his chest tightened. He looked at Raymond Dailey and felt sick to his stomach, but mustered up a smile and commented, "I see you have met Mr. Dailey."

He saw Isabella's expression change as she accused Raymond, "I thought you did not know Lucas."

"I do remember him now. It seems age has messed with my mind," Raymond said with an annoying grin on his selfish lips. Lucas knew what Raymond really was, and was appalled that Isabella would even think of speaking to such a man. Lucas took Isabella's hand and looked into Raymond's eyes and swallowed, "I believe it is time for me and my friends to get going."

"We have just arrived, Lucas," Isabella commented as she looked at him and then to Raymond.

"I believe it best we go, Isabella," he said with a controlled tone.

Lucas never liked Raymond Dailey and he certainly did not like him now. He had the mind to tell Mr. Dailey to beat it or he would rough him up for good. However, a reunion was not a proper place for such things. There was a feeling Lucas got when he was around Raymond that could not be explained. All the more, he did not want sweet Isabella hanging around a man like Raymond Dailey. He felt Irene behind him and told her it was time to go, so Irene convinced Isabella to go with them. Before he left, Lucas looked into Raymond's cobra–like eyes trying to send a warning that he would protect Isabella at all costs. The women left before him, but he was behind them the whole way home, watching the many intoxicated men on the street. He knew that Isabella would be upset with him for cutting off her conversation with Raymond, but it was for the best. She was such a wonderful woman with much potential and a caring heart and Lucas did not want to see her wasted on a fool like Raymond; she was worth much more than that.

A day passed and Irene washed the plates in the small kitchen as Lucas straightened the living area that contained one old couch and two rocking chairs, both made by their grandfather. Lucas took the trash and put it in the bin by the sink. He looked at his sister and offered, "I'll do them."

She gave him a smile and thanked her older brother for his help, and again for the roof over her head. Since their parents died, Lucas and Irene had been on their own, but that did not phase the two for long. Lucas was successful enough to live in the city, and Irene was one of the most desired ladies in town. Lucas took off his coat, tie, dress shoes, and vest as he rolled up his sleeves to work. The food came off the dishes well, except for the pan, which needed extra scrubbing. As he placed the pan in the water to soak he heard a loud slam, which he presumed to be their front door, and a voice saying, "I think I'm stuck for good, Irene!"

From the moment the first word trickled out of her mouth, Lucas could tell that the voice was Isabella Archer's. He shook his head and continued to work on the pan, all the while listening to the conversation in the room behind him.

Isabella glanced at the faded wallpaper that covered the wall behind Irene as she waited for her to reply. Isabella looked at her friend's confused expression and explained further. "I went on a date with Raymond tonight."

Irene looked at her with a small, but noticeable frown and began to ask Isabella why she went with Raymond to begin with. Isabella could think of no answer, but that he seemed nice. However, she came out with, "I think I could marry a man like him."

Irene shook her head as her blonde curls bounced, "You barely know him, Isabella."

"That does not matter if it is love and you know it," she replied with a bitter tone. Isabella sat by Irene and asked, "Do you not trust me?"

Irene batted her eyes. "I don't trust him."

"You don't know him, Irene," Isabella argued, raising her voice.

"Neither do you," a voice said from behind.

Isabella turned around to see Lucas, someone whom she had momentarily forgotten resided in the same apartment as Irene. Her face blushed for an unknown reason, but possibly because she knew she was wrong. The two friends looked at each other for a moment until Lucas joined them in the living room. Isabella waited for Lucas to give her a lecture on how to behave or what to do, but was shocked to hear him ask, "Why do you love him?"

He rested his elbows on his knees and his head on his hands, but Isabella knew that inside he was dying to scold her. However, she looked to Irene and then to Lucas. Irene gave a shrug and motioned for her to answer the question that was suffocating the three of them. Isabella gave a simple huff and replied, "He treats me well."

Lucas rolled his eyes and Isabella knew a sermon was about to spew out of his mouth. He lifted his head and asked, "Is that all?"

Isabella was stunned again and rubbed her hands on her sequined dress. She looked at Irene and asked, "What do you think Irene?"

Isabella watched as Irene cleared her throat and folded her hands to say, "I agree with Lucas, but the choice is yours. I would suggest you choose wisely."

"Is that it then?", Isabella asked, looking at her friends for a smile, "I thought you would be happy for me."

Lucas stood with a sigh and rubbed his eyes. "I do not like him, Isabella, and I do not condone your relationship."

Fury raged through her as she felt heat in the pit of her stomach. "Who are you to condone anything I do, Lucas. You are my friend, not my chaperone or my brother, and you are certainly not my father."

Isabella watched as Lucas turned to face her with wide and violent eyes. It was then when she immediately wished she could take back every word she had said.

Lucas' heart stopped for a moment as he looked at Isabella with the weight of silence surrounding them. He looked at her soft brown eyes and wished that he did not love her so much that he hated every inch of her in that moment. Lucas took a breath and breathed out with a huff, seeing just how sorry Isabella was. He looked at her almost perfect complexion and bit back a smile. "I did not presume I was any of those things, Isabella. I just want what is best for you."

He could see the sorrow in her eyes when she asked him to forget what she said, but he couldn't, because either he gave her those impressions or she thought them up herself. Lucas shook his head and focused on his anger for her to prevent himself from cracking a smile. "I think it would be best if you left."

Isabella blinked back evident tears and waived goodbye to Irene, who walked her to the door and made sure she had a way home. Lucas, on the other hand, sat down and laughed as he ran his hands though his hair. Isabella was his dearest friend and he could not see her hurt, but she was too stubborn a match for even him. Isabella, he knew, would have to figure things out the hard way.

Day seventy-four passed as Christmas rolled around, and Lucas still worried for Isabella. Christmas was always a sadder time for Lucas, because seeing his friends happily married still shook him up. He, Fred, and Raymond were the last of his friends who were still single, but Lucas had a feeling that that would soon change. As he watched Isabella grow more and more attached to Raymond, the more he desired to wipe Raymond from the planet for good. He tucked in his shirt and buttoned his vest, still numb to the fact that another Christmas had come. He called Irene into the room to help him with his tie and noticed her light pink gown with silver stitching and beading. Her white gloves went past her elbows, her white hat sat on her blonde head, and white pearls hung around her neck. "You'd look like a flapper if you had shorter hair."

"I am ignoring you, Lucas. It is the newest style. Things are changing."

"Things have already changed," he said in a crisp tone.

Lucas watched his sister's playful smile harden into a non-responsive scowl. "Isabella can make her own mistakes, and you need to make a few of your own too."

Lucas sat on the couch and asked, "What does that mean?"

His sister sat with him and took his hand, "You are so much better than her, Lucas. You have so much to offer the world."

"So does she."

Lucas watched as Irene pressed her lips together and asked, "Lucas, I'm not blind. I know you loved her back then when we were kids, but you moved on years ago, so why is this bothering you now?"

"He's a bad man, Irene," Lucas replied as he shook his head with regret.

"Trust that Isabella will make the right decision," Irene encouraged as she motioned for Lucas to follow her. He stood up and walked out of the apartment and toward the annual Christmas party he knew Isabella and Raymond were going to attend.

Isabella ran her hands down her black low-waisted dress and took Raymond's arm. She looked into his promising eyes and saw his strange behavior. She knew that something was wrong with him, but she could not tell what he was thinking. Isabella looked forward and met eyes with Lucas as she passed him. She saw his eyes glaze over and wondered if she was making the right choice in staying with Raymond, even when her closest friend detested the match. Lucas had a keen eye for personalities, she knew that. So, why had she not taken his advice and never even entertained the idea of Raymond Dailey? She looked at Raymond's profile and his confidence outshone any flaw he could possibly have. Isabella felt as if she was making the right choice; Raymond obviously loved her which was more than any other man had ever done for her.

As the night went on, she could sense Raymond getting stranger and stranger. She scanned the room for faces she knew and saw Irene and Fred, Irene's man, talking together in a corner of the room. Her heart warmed at the sight and she was happy for her friend. She knew that Irene had waited many years to finally be with Fred. Isabella remembered the tears that came after his departure for school four years ago. As she looked at them now, she envied every ounce of pain Irene felt all those years.

Isabella looked at Lucas, who seemed to be watching her and wondered what life would be like with him. Just as her thoughts turned to Lucas, Raymond tapped her on the shoulder and took her hand. With no time to think, she was up on the stage with Raymond and the jazz band. As they finished "Everybody Loves My Baby", the jazz band fell silent and all Isabella could hear was the sound of her beating heart. She had never been one for crowds, and she had a feeling what was going to happen next. Isabella watched as

Raymond took a knee in front of her as her stomach churned. She closed her eyes and focused on her breathing as Raymond asked, "Isabella Archer, my friend, my dream, my love, will you do me the honor and marry me?"

Isabella was frozen and she looked into the eyes of the man she thought she loved, but knew that Lucas' warning eye was on her. Was a life of happiness worth the risk of losing a friend like Lucas and the support of a friend like Irene? Happiness was in front of her, she had been proposed to, an offer that would most likely never come again. So, she took Raymond's hands and helped him up as she replied, "Yes."

Lucas dropped his glass as the crowd around him began to cheer. He watched as Raymond put his hands around Isabella and kissed her lips. She kissed him back and with every kiss Lucas grew more and more uncomfortable. He took a breath to hold back his anger as he walked out of the mansion and into the garden adjacent to it. The night was cool, but he did not mind the cold. He took the rocks that laid at his feet and began to throw them at the walls of Raymond's large home. Lucas' chest ached and his breath was hard to catch as he chunked rocks at the future for wich he once dreamed. He could not keep his eyes from pouring out the tears he had not wanted to spill for years. Lucas needed to feel the pain of Isabella's loss; if he didn't, it would be as if she had never gone. Lucas lost track of time as he stood there in his grief and anger. There was a small whimper of a voice behind him and he looked back and saw Irene's soft look of sorrow in her understanding eyes. He swallowed and wiped his face with his sleeve, getting rid of any evidence that he had been crying. Lucas cleared his throat and commented, "There is nothing to see here."

He watched as Irene approached him slowly, timid that he might hurt her, which he never would. She folded her arms across her stomach as she asked, "What's eating you?"

He rolled his eyes and let out a sigh, "Just taking a walk to clear my head."

"She left with him an hour ago, Lucas," Irene said with the tenderness only a sister could share.

Lucas let out a sarcastic laugh, "Why did he leave? This is his house."

He rubbed his forehead as Irene came closer to him with widening eyes, realizing, "You never did get over her, did you?"

He gave a small bittersweet smile as he wiped his sweaty brow, "I love her. I have always loved her and I always will."

Irene shook her head, "Lucas, she is getting married. There comes a time when we all have to move on."

He began to raise his voice, "There is no moving on, Irene. I love her and that poison will cripple me until the day I die."

"She had no part in it, Lucas," Irene defended.

Lucas was so infuriated that he threw a rock at the wall and turned to his sister calmly stating through his teeth, "She had everything to do with it, and you know it. She chose him when I told her it was a bad idea. Am I not the clear choice? Have I not done everything right? There is no use in moving on, you see, because we were nowhere to begin with."

"That is your fault, not her's," Irene said as she stepped away from her brother.

Tears filled Lucas' eyes. He shook his head as he sat on the ground. The pounding in his forehead increased and he knew that it was he who had made the biggest mistake. He looked up at his sister and commented, "I did this."

Irene sat with her brother and replied, "You have to forget her, Lucas."

He looked in his sister's comforting eyes and confessed, "That's just it, I can't."

THE TRUTH
Christlike Love

As I finished covering the hole, sweat poured from my forehead. I could not tell if I was worried or if the hot summer day had just taken it out of me. I walked back inside to wash off my hands and get a drink of water. Wanting to get the smell off of my clothes, I stuck them in the washer and began to heat up the shower. Not having shaved the night before, I decided my face needed the change. By the time I was out of the shower and clean, my doorbell rang. I answered it, reluctantly. Three officers in uniform asked if my name was Derek Madison, and I wished it wasn't.

They handcuffed me after I told them my name. As they lead me to the car, I could hear the radio saying that they had found the killer and that everything would be okay. I never thought anyone would ever talk about me that way. I honestly did not mean to hurt those girls.

The holding cell was bland and boring, but I was thankful I was the only one in there that night. People did not like me, which was new for me. Normally, everyone wanted to be my friend and I was happy to be friends with everyone.

The interviews were brutal, but I asked for a lawyer right away. I'm pretty sure that meant they knew I did something wrong, but I didn't care. I didn't want to go to jail. I didn't want to die. No one does. I just got carried away and didn't know what had come over me. Once I started I couldn't stop. I hoped they would't make me talk on the stand. I hated speaking in front of people.

My lawyer didn't like me, I could tell. I explained everything to him and told him exactly where they were all buried. I hoped this would get me life in prison, because I was looking at capital punishment. My lawyer said that there may not be all that much he could do, because the evidence clearly pointed toward me.

The trial was humiliating. My mother was there crying loud tears that rang in my head for the rest of the day. I saw the girls' families staring at me. The moms were crying and the fathers looked as if they would take me down with a shotgun right then and there. I would not blame them if they did, honestly. The jury was gone for three hours trying to decide my fate. I plead guilty so there was nothing really to decide on the account of my innocence. I was guilty and I prayed that by saying that they could see my remorse.

Now, the only reason I am telling this story is because of what happened duing my sentencing. I was standing there with my lawyers in a jumpsuit and chains as the judge looked over my paperwork. There were less people in the room during this part of my inevitable dance toward execution. My throat was dry and my hands were hot. The judge looked at me through his ancient glasses and sentenced me to death row. My mother cried as the girls' parents clapped and gave one another hugs. Just as I was about to be lead out, a man sitting in the back of the room approached the stand and said, "Take me instead, I did it."

My heart was racing at this point and I can truthfully say that tears were running down my face. I looked at the man, a man I had never seen before. He looked at me with such sympathy and understanding, like he had been in my exact same place. They did some more paperwork while I waited with my lawyer, but all I could think of was why. Why had this man given his life for my pathetic one? I was not a king, the president, a millionaire, or even a current movie star. I was just a small town boy with a big mistake hanging around my neck.

They sat the man down and then began to sift through the evidence piece by piece. With each victim's name they called out, I could see the man taking on their murders as if he had committed them himself. I looked at my lawyer who sat in astonishment, happy that his client was found not guilty for once.

The time came for them to carry the man out of the room and into my holding cell. As they rushed him past me and fastened his chains, I looked into his forgiving eyes and saw someone who saw me as a man with a mistake, not a mistake of a man.

"Why are you doing this?" I asked as he turned around to look at me.

"I am doing this for you."

I could not believe my ears. I looked at him and whispered, "I don't understand. We both know I did this. I do not deserve this, please, don't waste your life."

"It is not me who is wasting my life."

"Please, why are you doing this? I did this."

The man looked at me with such tenderness that I cannot explain to you what it felt like or what it looked like.

"That is why it is called grace."

I went home that night with a formal apology from the police force and my regular clothes, hallelujah. When I looked out of my window, I saw the nine small graves that had been dug up. I imagined their faces in my mind and for the first time I was ashamed of the man I had become.

My heart was changed that night. Those girls were people, just like me. That nice man was a person, like me. Why would I let him take my place? I did not deserve for him to take my place, I knew that. However, it then occurred to me that I never asked him to, he did it on his own for me. It was a gift. I had been given the greatest gift and was too ashamed and guilty to even accept what was freely given to me. He chose to save me. Me! Of all people in the world, that man traded his life for mine. It was something I never could shake away.

I decided to go to his execution just to see what it was like. There was something inside of me that was curious to see if he would go through with it. They walked him out of the hallway and into the room. All that separated us from him was thick glass. The mothers and fathers of the girls were there, but I had dyed my hair so they would not recognize me. I chose blonde, because it seemed fitting for my new lease on life. They laid him down on a table that looked like something out of "Frankenstein". They spread out his arms and tied down his hands and feet so that he would not injure himself further, I assume. There were three men in the room with him. One that looked to be a doctor, and two prison guards, the toughest two men I have seen to date. The doctor reddied the machines and prepared the injection. I looked at the man who had taken my place and saw the bruises from the other inmates that shared his fate. No one likes people who hurt children, even inmates. While watching him, I felt sick to my stomach, knowing that that would be me on the table if it were not for this man. As I shook my head and wiped a tear from my eye he mouthed the words, "I forgive you."

Before I had time to reply, the doctor had injected him with the deadly drug. I watched as they placed a black blanket over his body and closed the viewing curtains. The people poured out of the room, some with a smile and some still mourning, but I was left standing numb to the fact that I had been forgiven and my life had been spared.

"For while we were still weak, at the right time Christ died for the ungodly. For one will scarcely die for a righteous person—though perhaps for a good person one would dare even to die—but God shows his love for us in that while we were still sinners, Christ died for us."
Romans 5:6–8

"Love is patient, love is kind. It does not envy, it does not boast, it is not proud. It does not dishonor others, it is not self-seeking, it is not easily angered, it keeps no record of wrongs. Love does not delight in evil but rejoices with the truth. It always protects, always trusts, always hopes, always perseveres."
1 Corinthians 13:4–7

"Beloved, let us love one another, for love is from God, and whoever loves has been born of God and knows God. Anyone who does not love does not know God, because God is love."
1 John 4:7–8

"For God so loved the world that he gave his one and only Son, that whoever believes in him shall not perish but have eternal life. For God did not send his Son into the world to condemn the world, but to save the world through him."
John 3:16–17

"We love because he first loved us."
1 John 4:19

ABOUT THE AUTHOR

Megan Karr attends Missouri State University where she studies both Theatre and Creative Writing. Growing up in Tomball, Texas, a short distance from Houston, Megan participated in musical and theatrical performances throughout high school. Her love of writing did not bloom until she began writing her first novel at the age of fourteen. Megan is grateful for all of the friends and family that have supported and encouraged her throughout her life. Through her writing, Megan seeks to challenge and inspire readers toward courage in love, faith, and purity.

Made in the USA
Middletown, DE
01 July 2015